A Promise to be Kept

By Isaac Smythia

A Promise to be Kept

Print ISBN: 978-1-7923-7447-0

Digital ISBN: 978-1-7923-7448-7

Acknowledgements

I am grateful to friends who added beautiful color to *A Promise to be Kept*. I borrowed the Winberry surname from some dear Tennessean friends. Pastors Chad, Bill, and Jonathan loaned their names to enhance the story for those who know them well and for those who have never met them. Additionally, Bill was so kind as to read each chapter as it was finished. His comments motivated me to continue.

Gordon, Beth, Sharon, Ruthy, and Jonathan reviewed the manuscript. Doug, a Civil War historian and reenactor, helped me keep Jaime's story true to the record of the conflict that divided our country for four tumultuous years.

My editor, Dawn, worked tirelessly editing and revising the text, always with an eye toward a readable story that takes the readers on a journey that will hopefully bring them closer to God. Special thanks to Obie Harrup III for the cover design and to Neil Ruda for formatting the print and digital versions of the book.

Thanks to the love of my life after Jesus Christ, Terry. Her support through all my projects keeps me writing. Finally, thanks to my Heavenly Father for the faithful promise He made to me and has kept for almost fifty years now. It is the foundation for *A Promise to be Kept*.

Table of Contents

For Jason and Brianne

Raising and releasing you are some of my best memories. Remember, there is nothing more important than serving Jesus!

Prologue

The rebel yell echoed across the hills as the gray-clad men on Seminary Ridge, Gettysburg, their battle flags unfurled, prepared to charge down the hill, across the valley, and up the opposite hill to Cemetery Ridge. But instead of the roar of supporting artillery, the buzz of minié balls, and the thunder of cavalry, this charge came only with the subdued sounds of elderly veterans of the Army of Northern Virginia straining and groaning as they retraced their fifty-year-old steps. Many used canes. Others had to be helped to make their way to their awaiting opponents whose own flags flapped in the hot, July afternoon wind. Each step was alive with memories of sounds, smells, and images of the day that had changed the course of a war and a nation. Ghosts of fighters long gone marched alongside them in this last tribute by those who had fought so many years before.

Reaching "The Angle," a short stone wall that marked the farthest incursion of Pickett's charge, the gray-haired combatants were met, not with muskets or sabers, but with outstretched hands and, in some cases, open arms that received them with friendship and even tears. For a few, Thursday, July 3, 1913, marked the end of a long journey.

Chapter 1

The Dream

Tuesday, July 1, 1913

The table was just as he remembered it. Worn and warm, unpainted but stained from years of use. It had a slight wobble that had always prompted him to keep an elbow on the left-hand corner to hold it down. He pulled out the once blue, cane-bottomed chair and sat down. The back of the chair was made of three slats that fit his back as though they were made for him.

Henry stepped out of the shadows and sat across the table. Henry's skin was the color of hot coffee with a splash of milk. His beard was thin and short, a mixture of white and black that matched his hair. Dark eyes that were at once kind, but piercing, looked out from under thick eyebrows and the three deep age lines that crossed his forehead. Henry's lips hid bright teeth that flashed whenever he spoke or laughed.

Henry sat comfortably in his chair, resting a half-open hand on a well-worn Bible that lay on the tabletop. His exposed wrist bore the dark shadow of some past binding.

They would talk as friends for what seemed like hours. The depth of Henry's knowledge and wisdom was impressive. The man never lacked for an answer or an opinion that was rendered without hesitation. Yet recalling their conversations afterwards was like trying to grasp the morning fog as it swirled away and vanished. It was not the content that mattered as much as that their conversations occurred at all. There were no awkward silences, no searching for a safe way to say something. No subject was off limits, but neither was there pressure to discuss anything difficult. Like slavery. Henry was a slave, and *slaves didn't sit across tables to speak with sons of white pastors.*

Jaime Winberry's eyes jerked open in the semi-dark of a new morning. He stared up at the off-white canvas tent ceiling that stretched above the army-issue cot on which he had slept. Sounds of the just-stirring camp began to rise with the summer sun.

Jaime took his time pulling on his shoes before he hobbled outside the tent. A gray, tattered campaign hat sat on his head. A frazzled jacket hung loosely on his stooped, thin shoulders. Hundreds of identical tents reflected the morning sun throughout the encampment. It was the first time Jaime had walked the fields of Gettysburg in fifty years. He had heard that over fifty thousand veterans, both blue and gray, were gathered to commemorate the battle that had turned the tide of the Civil War. Jaime was one of only eight thousand or so members of Lee's Army of Northern Virginia who had come. Most were gone; others just couldn't face reliving the memories. Neither Jaime nor the horde of white-haired warriors camped with him had any idea that in just a year the world would be thrown into "the war to end all wars."

Jaime's thoughts trailed back over the years to his very first conversation with Henry. He had not yet celebrated his thirteenth birthday. He remembered standing at the curtain that separated his parent's bed from the rest of the cabin. John and Martha Winberry pastored the Ketoctin Baptist Church in Loudoun County. Twenty thousand souls populated the beautiful rolling hills of that part of Northern Virginia of which 1,200 were free blacks, 5,500 were slaves, and 670 were slaveholders.

Young Jaime hesitated, summoning the courage to speak to his mother. She was in bed, pregnant with his sister, Mary. Four-year-old Jeremiah played quietly in the corner with a couple of half-shucked ears of dried corn.

"Mother, are dreams real?"

Martha was only sixteen years her boy's elder, but twenty-eight years of hard work and now a third baby on the way hung heavy upon her body. She looked long at her son and smiled before patting the patchwork quilt that her own mother had made for her. Her son quickly hopped up beside her just as he had when she used to tell him the stories of Baby Moses or Daniel in the lions' den.

"Why would you ask that, Jaime Love?" she replied, using her special name for her boy. An ever so slight lilt in her voice revealed her Irish roots.

In response, words poured out of Jaime's heart, stopping only when he tried to remember what Henry and he had talked about.

"Hmm, how did you know his name was Henry?"

Young Jaime's face puckered like a persimmon as he pondered. "I don't remember ... but it was Henry. I just know it. And Momma, he looked me right in the eye like he was somebody, and like I was somebody too. And Momma, it was real! Just as real as you an' me talkin' right here."

Martha looked at her son intently. "Your Great-Grandfather Hezekiah Smith was said to have had dreams from God, just like Joseph in the Old Testament and the wise men in the New Testament. And he was a pastor like your papa and a chaplain in the Continental Army."

Jaime slipped off the bed and leaned against the wooden post at its foot as he considered his mother's words. "God?" he replied. "What do ya think God wants to tell me?"

"Jaime Love, that is something you will just have to find out for yourself."

The not-yet-a-man walked out the door of the small cabin and around the corner to the nearby tree line. Jaime had been clearing underbrush and small trees there for kindling and firewood since he was old enough to hold a hatchet. His father had left the half-acre stand of hickory that was interspersed by three large live oak trees. It was like a park. The farthest oak held Jaime's secret place. A robust limb bent low enough for him to swing up and seat himself in the niche where it joined the main trunk, out of sight from the cabin.

"God," he began, not knowing where this conversation was going to take him. "I wish I knew what You wanted to tell me." There was no answer other than wind playing through the oak leaves, and the "twit, twit, twit" of an unseen cardinal. But something took place deep inside James Allen Winberry. He didn't recognize it at the time, but a door had opened in his heart, and Someone had entered.

Chapter 2

Goose Creek

Friday, August 12, 1859

Five years passed before Jaime saw Henry again. Almost every Friday night, Pastor John Winberry slipped into the darkness, usually returning with the breaking dawn. There was talk of some Baptist pastors who were illegally teaching slaves to read and write, but Jaime's father never talked about his late-night activities.

At seventeen, Jaime felt he was man enough to find out what his father was doing. Standing at almost six feet, Jaime was two fingers taller than his father and most of the men he knew. The young man was slim, well-muscled, with a thick head of brown hair that was marked with a small patch of blond just above his neck and behind his right ear. His mother teased him that it was from an angel's kiss when he was born. His gray-green eyes matched hers. The faded fork-shaped scar on the inside of his right forearm bore testimony to the fact that you should not play with the cat through the broken slats of the pickle barrel, especially if you might catch your arm on a hidden nail.

Pastor John, as he was known by both the white and black communities, loved to sing and laugh. He made up songs about his children that made them first cringe and then smile. Martha laid out his clothes for him and often chided her husband for the crumbs and stains on his shirts. John Winberry's looks were unremarkable. Most of his friends and family couldn't tell you the color of his eyes. His hair, what he had of it, would have been described as just brown. He often wondered aloud what he had done to win Martha's heart. Jaime never heard his mother's response, but never forgot her smiles.

Jaime followed his father into the darkness, staying just far enough behind to see the faint glow of the closed-in metal lantern that Pastor John used to light his path. Somewhere along the banks of Goose Creek, the light went out. Jaime froze in place, listening for the sound of his father's feet. Nothing. The half-moon gave the young man just enough light to make it to a large cottonwood tree beside the creek. He sat down, leaned against the trunk, and listened again. All he could hear was the sound of mosquitoes buzzing around his ears. Eventually, Jaime's head and eyes grew heavy.

He opened them to see Henry sitting at the table with an arm outstretched, motioning for him to sit down in his faded blue chair. Jaime should have been startled, but there was no startle in him, just a feeling of warmth and welcome. He sat. His elbow found its way to the left corner of the table, provoking a nod and smile from Henry. How long they talked and the content of their conversation were lost the moment he opened his eyes.

Jaime awoke to the sound of furtive murmuring from along the path his father had taken. A faint light, perhaps from another lamp, led the way for three shadows that moved cautiously in the direction of the cottonwood. Every so often the lamp raised as if they were looking for something. Then it stopped just beyond the tree and began to move down the bank toward the creek.

Jaime hadn't noticed it before, but a small raft lay hidden beneath a pile of brush alongside the water. Someone set the lamp down to move the brush and untie the raft. Jaime jerked as he saw the face in the light of the lamp. "Henry?" he called out in a voice that sounded much louder than he had intended. All movement around the raft stopped. No one breathed as Jaime stood and walked over to the lamp. He picked it up and held it near the terrified eyes of the man he took for Henry. It could have been Henry's younger brother, but his face held none of Henry's peaceful dignity. Jaime shone the lamp on a pregnant woman with one foot on the raft. Another man, still in the shadows, was lifting a large branch. Its leaves had provided cover for the homemade craft. Jaime took a step back and squatted on his haunches, unsure what to do.

"They're runaways." The voice of his father from the path just above broke the brittle silence. "Why don't you come up here with me, Son." Jaime set the lamp down and climbed the slight grade to his father.

The trio cast the remaining branches off the raft, grabbed the lamp, and pushed off into the creek. Goose Creek flowed into the Potomac River which formed the boundary between Virginia and Maryland. Maryland was a slave state but was also home for many free blacks. More importantly, free Pennsylvania lay just fifty miles or so away.

Father and son stood quietly as they watched the raft drift out into the stream where it was swallowed by the night. Then John turned and headed down the path, careful steps lit by the dim light of his lantern. Jaime stayed behind him until they reached the road that would take them home. Side by side now, their silence was broken only by the pad of their steps on the hard-packed surface.

Jaime's mind raced back and forth between his dream and the image of the escapees. He didn't know what to do, what to say. Virginia and slavery were tightly intertwined, a strong rope that had held the state together for two hundred years. But the still-fresh memories of the night were proof that the rope was fraying. The young man looked across at the shadow that was his father. He could just distinguish the outline of his father's head as it turned toward him with what may have been a smile.

The pair saw a light in the window of their home as they turned off the road and onto the path that led to the three steps of the small, covered porch of their cabin. The front door opened just as they were stomping the dew off their boots.

Jaime's mother was still in her white, ankle-length nightgown. The long braid of her hair rested on her left shoulder. Martha gave her husband a quick kiss and turned to her son. "Well, Jaime Love," her voiced lilted. "You've had quite a night, I think. Come inside, both of you. I'll put on some coffee. But mind you don't wake the children." And just like that, Jaime became a man.

Chapter 3

Lizzie

Sunday, July 14, 1861

"No! I don't understand!" Lizzie Houghton's voice broke through the wall of silence that had followed Jaime's announcement. He had enlisted in the Eighth Virginia Infantry, showing up at her family home wearing his newly issued uniform. The young soldier's heavy woolen shirt was buttoned at the top and scratched against his neck. Jaime wore no tie as his gray jacket buttoned to the top as well. He wore his own shoes and undergarments as well as socks handknit by his mother.

"What's not to understand, Elizabeth Anne?" His annoyance was communicated by his tone and the use of her full name instead of the nickname she usually went by. "We're about to be invaded by the Union army, and you better believe they will cross the Potomac and come through Loudoun County!"

Seventeen-year-old Elizabeth Anne Houghton was a fireball stuffed into a five-foot three-inch package, all topped by a thick pile of wavy brown hair that no matter the bun or braids she used to tame it, always rebelled with a strand that fell over her left eyebrow. Her eyes were either brown and green or green and brown, depending on the light and her mood. Her nose was at once delicate and defiant with just a slight upward turn at the tip. Her lips and cheeks ... Jaime had his own description of every part of Lizzie's face, neck, and hands that he kept tucked away in his heart. He also had his own description of her temper—dry gunpowder! It never took much for it to go off, and that usually in his face.

Neither Jaime nor Lizzie could remember not having the other in his or her life. The Houghton's were faithful members of Ketoctin Baptist Church. Her father, Elijah, had served as deacon off and on over the years. Jaime and Lizzie had stopped treating each other as just childhood friends after riding together three summers earlier. Lizzie had fallen from her pony and been dragged for about twenty feet. Jaime had thrown himself from his own mount onto hers and wrestled her pony to a standstill. The doctor from Leesburg did a good job of setting and splinting her ankle. He told Lizzie's parents that without the boy's quick thinking, they might have lost their only child, born in their later years. The slight limp from her bad ankle was only noticeable when she was very tired. Or angry.

Now Lizzie stomped across the porch, her limp noticeable, and sat down on the steps beside the young man she had yet to tell she loved. "Have you talked to Henry about this?" Lizzie whispered harshly into Jaime's ear. The young man's eyes flared. His own reserve of anger usually had a long fuse, but she had brought up the dreams he had told no one else about except his mother, and that only once.

The truth was, Jaime could not begin to untangle his divided feelings. The Ordinance of Secession that would take Virginia out of the Union had passed just three months before on April 17, 1861, by a vote of eighty-five to fifty-five. Both of Loudoun County's representatives, John Janney and John A. Carter, had voted against secession. That vote was followed by a ratification ballot by each county. Loudoun County's vote was 1,626 to 726 in favor of secession.

The northwestern counties of the Commonwealth that lay on the west side of the Blue Ridge mountains voted strongly to remain in the Union. The pro-Union counties then set up what they called the Restored Government of Virginia in Wheeling as an alternative to the Confederate state government based in Richmond. Like a funnel suddenly turned upside down, Loudoun County became the northernmost access point to Virginia. The Potomac River offered eight places to cross into Loudoun County from Union Maryland.

Jaime had been torn as he watched his friends join the Eighth Virginia Infantry in waves. April 19, the militia known as the Hillsboro Border Guards became Company A. On May 13, Company D, Champe Rifles formed. Just over two weeks later, Captain Mandley

Hampton formed Company E, followed by the Blue Ridge Boys of Company F on June 19. Everyone was issued a uniform, a Springfield Model 1855 rifle, and had moved into the growing number of military camps that popped up across the hills of Loudoun County.

Jaime wasn't sure what an abolitionist was. However, every time he saw slaves working the fields or walking the roads, the young man thought of Henry and of the three terrified runaways on Goose Creek. But he also loved his country. For Jaime, his country was bordered by the Potomac River to the north and the Blue Ridge Mountains to the west. He had listened carefully to the multitude of speakers who had come to Loudoun County prior to the vote for secession with warnings of the threat to the Commonwealth of Virginia's rights and the pending danger from the Union Army.

By Sunday service on July 7th, there was not one man between the ages of eighteen and forty, other than Jaime, in the pews when his father stepped behind the pulpit to share the Word of God. Jaime closed his eyes and prayed as he never had before. "Oh, Jesus, I don't know what to do, and I have to do something!" As he prayed, the memory of his friend, Henry, sitting across that old table faded and was replaced by the image of an invading blue army destroying everything Jaime knew and loved.

The following Saturday found Jaime in Leesburg, part of company H, the Potomac Grays, under the command of Captain J. Morris Wampler. Just after changing into his uniform, the new private received permission to take Sunday to say goodbye to his loved ones.

Mother cried. Father brought the family together in a circle and prayed God's protection upon their firstborn. Six-year-old Mary grabbed her big brother's legs and almost made him trip. Jeremiah began talk of killin' bluebellies until their father sternly quieted him down.

"James Allen," Pastor John began, "I know you have to do what you feel to be right. But remember one thing. No matter what happens, nothing is more important than serving Jesus."

Head bowed, his son replied with meaning in his words, "Yes, sir." For Jaime, serving Jesus was something he naturally did just by being the pastor's son. The memory of family prayers, his father in the pulpit, and his mother reading her Bible by the light of the fireplace were deeply carved into the foundation of his life. He still didn't understand what God wanted to say to him through his dreams. His father had described his son's relationship with Jesus as a seedling well planted, fertilized, and cultivated. The rest was now in God's hands.

As they walked out the door together, Martha slid her arm around her boy's waist and pulled him in close. "Son, you'll be heading over to see Lizzie I think, no?" He nodded and released his mother's embrace as he started down the porch stairs. The young man was only two steps away when he heard her voice again. "Every day, Jaime Love! Every day will I lift your name to God till He brings you back to me!" He turned around and grabbed both parents in one last hug.

Jaime had hoped for a similar reaction from Lizzie, but to no avail. "Of all people, Lizzie! Of all people, you should understand. I'm not doin' this for me. I'm doin' this for Mother and Father, for Mary and Jeremiah, … and for you!"

He quickly stood to his feet at the bottom of the steps and turned to face Lizzie who was also standing, but on the second step. Their eyes met in silence as unspoken feelings rushed between them. Jaime reached out and brushed the wayward strand of hair from Lizzie's forehead. Lizzie hugged herself tightly, her chin quivering as she seemed to search for something to say. But words failed her. Jaime waited one long moment more before turning away to slowly retrace his steps up the path to Leesburg.

Lizzie stayed on the step, unmoving, until her bad ankle began to throb.

Chapter 4

Manassas

Sunday, July 21, 1861

"What are you writing?" Jaime asked, blowing over his steaming cup of coffee. The morning mists were just lifting off the fields of the Aris Buckner plantation where the Regiment had passed the night. Only four days after Jaime's enlistment, the Eighth Virginia had taken to the road. Talk was they were headed to Manassas. Jaime was still trying to get used to sleeping on the ground under the stars. Tents were a luxury of officers.

"It's a letter to my mother. Ya'll wanna hear what I told her?" replied Corporal George Donohoe. Jaime nodded, unsure of how much there was to write about yet. "We started out early," the young man began, only to be interrupted by another voice.

"Tell 'er we made eighteen mile yeste'day." It was Billy Ott. He had marched beside Jaime the previous day. Jaime was sure Billy's jaws must still be aching from yesterday's overuse, but that didn't stop him. Blue-eyed and blonde-haired William Baxter Ott had not yet begun to shave. If he tried hard, Billy may have reached five-foot-five inches tall. He looked like he had lied about his age to join the regiment. But he arrived in camp with a double barrel, 10-gauge shotgun, and a dangerous-looking Bowie knife, declaring he wanted to fight.

"It's my letter, Private!"

That caused Billy to clamp down on whatever words were about to sally forth from his mouth.

George began again. "We started early and after traveling until about two o'clock, we halted to take dinner which was composed of some bread that was so tough we could hardly pull it apart and some meat that was not much better." The corporal's look up at his audience was met by nods and grunts of agreement.

Jaime stood and stretched. Soon fires were extinguished, and bed rolls were draped over shoulders. Companies formed ranks and began moving south once again. Jaime's eyes involuntarily rolled as he looked to his right at his marching partner. Billy Ott, *again*! Fortunately, the regiment arrived at the outskirts of Manassas by midafternoon. Animated talk around the fires that night was of a quick fight, victory, and a return home in time for harvest. Over half of the soldiers in the Eighth Virginia were farm boys.

The next day saw the regiment deployed along Bull Run, a creek that skirted Manassas and emptied into the Potomac. They lay in the sun all day, expecting the enemy. This was to be the first real battle since Fort Sumter had fallen to the Confederacy in April. The insufferable July heat made the contrasting cool night spent in the fields a little more tolerable.

Jaime couldn't remember closing his eyes but welcomed Henry's visit. The young private had wondered if his friend would return now that he was wearing confederate gray. They talked about it, and many other things including … including. The only other remaining memory from their talk was Jaime's anxious heart being calmed, and something he told Henry about Billy Ott that made his friend throw back his head and laugh.

"God, I just don't understand it!" the confused young man prayed as he lay in the brown summer grass, his eyes still shut to the encroaching morning sun. Jamie's thoughts drifted back to his mother's words about Great-Grandpa Hezekiah, pastor and chaplain in the Continental Army eighty years before. "What are you trying to tell me? Who *is* Henry, and why is he my friend?" Once again the silence was broken only by the sounds of fellow soldiers stirring. Somewhere over Bull Run a red-tailed hawk screeched kee-eeeee-arr, kee-eeeee-arr.

The sharp crack of rifle fire began to reach his ears from somewhere not too far in the distance ahead of him. The noise continued to crescendo until it was joined by booms of what Jaime took to be artillery fire. It was the first time he had heard it. Soldiers looked at each other, wondering if they needed to run to the battle. Word came down from Captain Wampler that the Eighth Virginia was being held in reserve, but that Regimental Commander Colonel Eppa Hunton had appealed to General Beauregard. Soon the regiment was moving toward the sound of battle.

A battle line was formed behind the woods, northeast of Henry Hill. Chaplain Charles Linthicum rode to the front of the line and offered a prayer asking for God's protection and for victory. Jaime bowed his head to pray but wondered in his heart if he were on the right side of the battle lines.

Colonel Hunton took the chaplain's place facing the Eighth Virginia Infantry Regiment. The commander looked small on his horse and even smaller after he dismounted. Jaime watched as he pulled his sword from its scabbard. The Colonel had to grab his scabbard with his left hand so the last inches of the sword would clear.

"Eighth Virginia! Give 'em hell! Charge!" And Colonel Hunton rushed toward the lines of northern soldiers. His own soldiers' pent-up energy and hopes roared into a mighty battle cry as they charged toward the enemy lines. Jaime's doubts and fears were drowned in the tumult and noise of the moment. The northern lines broke, and their retreat quickly turned into a complete rout.

Word around the fires that night was that the regiment had suffered just six killed, another twenty-six wounded, and one soldier from Company C missing, probably captured. Jaime sat off by himself, his mind replaying the chaos of the battle. He wasn't sure he had killed anyone, but he may have wounded one or two. He did not share in the light banter of the other soldiers. They had fought, won, and more importantly, they had survived. Now they traded tales of their exploits, their animated faces lit by flickering flames.

Young Jaime rolled his blanket out under a nearby stand of loblolly pine. The thick accumulation of needles made for a softer bed than the bare ground. A short shadow broke the skyline. "Jaime, dat you?"

"It's me, Billy. What do you want?"

"I jus' lookin' for a good place ta sleep. Ya hear how many sogers I kilt?"

Jaime cut the boy-soldier off. "Billy, I'm tired and sore. If you want to bed down, there's plenty of room. But if you want to jaw all night, you just go back over to the fire."

The only response was the zipping sound of the string around sleeping blankets being removed, followed by a quiet rustle as they were rolled out over the needles. Then came an "Umph, umph!" as two pinecones were discovered under the blankets and quickly disposed of.

A few quiet minutes passed. Then, "Jaime … Jaime?"

"What is it, Billy?"

"I really not so sur' how many I actually kilt. It wa kinda hard to see through all dat dad gum gun smoke."

"Go. To. Sleep. Billy!"

Jaime hoped Henry might visit that night. He had lots of questions, but sleep evaded him till long after his fellow soldiers had turned in and the fires died down. When sleep finally came, it was dreamless.

Chapter 5

Little Davie

Monday, March 3, 1862

The sound of muffled voices drifted up the stairs of the Houghton home and into Lizzie's bedroom. Something was wrong. It was much too early for visitors. The rays of late winter sun had not yet brightened the horizon. The young woman brushed the sleep out of her eyes and pulled her door open a couple of inches. She could make out her father's voice. "Sam, you know that a lot of folk agree with you, but I and my family have chosen to remain behind. You will have to look elsewhere."

Samuel Means had been a successful grist miller and businessman in nearby Waterford. His mill had been the largest in Loudoun County. He was one of several

Quakers who lived in the northern part of the county, most of them abolitionists and pro-Union. The Confederates had wooed him for the use of his mill to fill the stomachs of its growing army. Sam had refused and fled to Maryland back in July when a warrant for his arrest had been issued. Now Sam was back as a scout for the Union Army, looking for pro-Union volunteers to help form what he called the Loudoun Rangers.

Lizzie snorted quietly to herself and thought, "You're not much of an antiviolence Quaker, Sam."

Sam Means' squeaky voice replied to her father's, "Elijah, you saw what they did. Seized everything I owned, almost thirty head of horses, all my hogs, not to mention the flour and meal at the mill. If it hadn't been for my business dealings with my brother in Maryland, I would have been left with nothing!"

"Sam, you put me in a terrible way. I'm too old to be sittin' in a saddle all day, sleepin' on the ground at night. And my Sally is in bed. The doctor tells us it's the beginning of consumption. All I have left is Lizzie."

At that Sam Means chuckled, "Well, I suspect she could hold her own in any fight."

Lizzie bit her lower lip to keep herself quiet.

Sam continued, "No, I see what you mean."

Lizzie's eyes grew heavy as she listened to shuffling feet. The two men finished their conversation, stood, and moved toward the door. Lizzie crept quietly back under her covers and closed her eyes.

A gunshot brought Lizzie out of bed and down the stairs to the open door. It felt like only minutes had passed, but outside in the early morning light were gray-uniformed cavalry soldiers. Their leader dismounted and stood face to face with her father. A small curl of smoke rose from the pistol of one of the mounted troops.

"Now, there's no need for that, Captain Jones," explained Lizzie's father. "As God in heaven is my witness, I will not lie to you. Sam Means is my friend, and he was here early this morning."

Captain William "Grumble" Jones had earned his nickname for his authoritarian ways with his cavalry troopers and anyone else he dealt with. "Sir, I would like to know what he was about and where he was off to after leaving your premises."

Elijah Houghton stood his ground solidly, a pillar of peace surrounded by violent, whirling winds. "Sam asked me to join him. I refused, and he left. Where he went after that, I do not know."

Captain Jones, obviously not satisfied with the older man's reply, took a menacing step towards him.

"That! Is! Enough!" Lizzie surprised herself with the strength in her voice as she launched her small form through the doorway and down the steps. The hastily grabbed broomstick in her hands rose like a sword ready to strike. The mounted horses around Grumble Jones involuntarily took a step back at the appearance of the little woman, still clad in her white winter nightgown, buttoned from the neck to the ankles, who stood barefoot and shivering before them. He could see her breath as she tried to blow a strand of hair from over her left eye.

The momentary silence was broken by the *click, click, click, click, click* of a dozen musket hammers being pulled back.

Captain Jones glanced over his shoulder. "At ease, Gentlemen!" He slowly examined the young woman, little more than a child, who had entered the fray much like David against Goliath. He had never pictured himself as Goliath before. He smiled inwardly and wondered just how many people saw him as an ogre. It wasn't such a bad thought. Could be useful …

Elijah Houghton sidestepped over to his daughter and gently took the broom out of her hands. He placed his arm around Lizzie's shoulders, giving her a light squeeze.

Lizzie slowly let out the breath she had been holding and began to blush in the realization that never had any man other than her father seen her in her nightgown.

"Sir," Grumble Jones redirected his attention to Elijah. "I mean you no harm. We are here in defense of our own daughters, wives, and way of life. Did you notice which direction Means took when he left your home?"

"It was still dark, Captain, but I think it was north," Lizzie's father replied, releasing his own long-held breath.

Captain William Jones stepped back and reached for the reins of his mount. "Thank you, sir. I ask that you please inform us if Samuel Means should stop by again. Lives are at stake." With that, he mounted and looked back at Lizzie. A smile broke out on his face. "Goliath indeed!" the man said just loud enough for Elijah and Lizzie to hear.

The young warrior's father looked up at the mounted man and back at his daughter twice before a broad smile of understanding spread across his own face.

"Alright, men. Let's move out!" The troopers quickly formed up, two by two, behind their leader who looked one more time at Lizzie and her father and snapped off a crisp salute.

The two stood in place until the horses were out of sight. Arm still around his daughter, Elijah turned and began to walk them both back up the stairs and into the house. "Well, little Davie, let's go check on your mother."

"Davie?" questioned the clueless girl.

"Never mind, Sweetheart. You shouldn't have come out like that. But all the same, I am proud of you, and I thank you!"

Chapter 6

Seven Pines

Friday, May 31, 1862

"You know, Henry, it's very hard for me to spend my nights with you and then not remember much of anything the next day."

"Well, Jaime, I am sorry you feel that way," replied the black man sitting comfortably opposite the young soldier. *"Would you rather I not visit you?"*

Jaime sat up in the faded blue chair, raising his elbow off the corner of the table. It wobbled a fraction of an inch before the young man settled himself down and brought the table back to its correct position.

"No, of course not. You are my friend. I ... I don't know what I would do if you were to leave. It's just that more and more I look at the slaves in the fields or walking down the road, and I think about you. What are we fighting for anyway? To protect our land and families or to keep these people enslaved? Jesus, help me. I don't know what to do." Jaime's growing frustration had begun to dominate their conversations every time they talked.

Henry said nothing but ran his fingers along the leather edges of the Bible that sat on the table under his hand. The silence dragged on for an uncomfortable moment.

Jaime broke the quiet. "You know that tomorrow we go back into battle. What should I do?"

"Watch out for Billy." Henry's answer came quickly, as if he had anticipated Jaime's question.

"Billy?" Jaime questioned in surprise, much louder than he intended.

"Yeah, Jaime. I be right here." Billy Ott's hand was on his shoulder, shaking him awake. "What you want?"

Jaime's memory was a fog once again, except for Henry's last instruction. "Nothin', Billy. I was just prayin' for you."

Billy lowered his face closer to his friend's until Jaime could see his bright blue eyes, open wide. "You praying to God 'bout me? Nobody's ever prayed for me that I know."

Jaime shook his head. "Well, I think I was more talkin' about you than actually praying for you."

"You was talking to Jesus 'bout me? What was you tellin' Him?" A note of panic crept into the soldier's voice and expression.

"No, no. It wasn't exactly Jesus I was talkin' to, but ..."

The call to muster interrupted Jaime just in time, and soon the soldiers of Eighth Virginia Infantry had fallen into formation and were marching in their assigned line of battle, just to the left of the Twenty-

Eighth Virginia Infantry and behind the Eighteenth and Nineteenth. This was to be a huge battle with one hundred thousand Union forces, led by General George B. McClellan, facing off against seventy-five thousand confederates under General Joseph E. Johnston.

For the first part of the afternoon, the regiment acquitted itself well. Companies E and A had joined company F in routing the Seventy-Second Pennsylvania's line. By 4:00 p.m., the Eighth Virginia was pulled off the line. However, the withdrawal turned into a fighting retreat as the Fifth and Sixth New Jersey Infantry Regiments poured relentless fire into their lines.

The buzz of minié balls, the crash of cannon fire, the smoke swirling around their heads, and the sloppy mud under their feet combined to leave the gray combatants in a state of confused chaos. It was run a few steps, stop, reload, and fire in the direction of the battle. Then repeat.

Billy grabbed Jaime's elbow and pointed him in the direction of a small log building up the hill and to the left. They jumped the split rail fence surrounding the building, opened the small wooden door on the near side, and ducked inside in hope of catching their breath. Instead, they faced raucous squawking, whirling wings, and flying feathers in near darkness. A dim and dusty ray of light peeked in through a shuttered and wire-covered window that faced the sound of battle.

"It's a chicken coop, Billy!"

"Yeah, I know. Ya gots any bullets left?" Both were reloading as fast as they could. Union minié balls slammed into the log walls, and a few penetrated. The poultry flew into a greater panic, adding to the young soldiers' terror.

Suddenly, Billy jerked and fell against a wall. "Jaime! Jaime! I'm shot!"

"Where'd they get'cha, Billy?"

"My head, I think! I can't feel nothin', but I got blood all over me. I'm shot, Jaime!" Billy's voice turned into a low wail as Jaime grabbed the boy's head and felt for the wound in the semidarkness.

"Can't find it, Billy. Where're you hit?"

"Don' know, Jaime, but I bleedin' somethin' awful! Owwwweeeee!"

"Okay, okay! Take a deep breath and settle down, Billy... Billy, shut up!"

Billy's cry quieted to a low whimper, enough to allow Jaime to search for the wound. Outside, the firing in their direction subsided a little, and the chickens, huddled in the back corner, began to quiet down.

Twice, Jaime ran his fingers through his friend's blood-soaked hair, over his ears, eyes, nose, and mouth. Nothin'. Then he felt something drip onto his hand from the nesting box just above them. He reached up over the box and felt feathers covering a warm mass. He grabbed the chicken's wing and lifted the body into what little light there was. A bullet had neatly taken off the head of a large, black Minorca rooster. It looked just like one of the Minorcas his folks raised back home. "Billy, you didn't get shot. This rooster here bled out all over you, that's all," Jaime explained as calmly as he could.

"I ain't shot? I'm gonna live? Thank You, Jesus! Thank you, Jaime! Ya prayed fer me, an' Jesus spared my life! Thank You, Jesus!"

"Okay, okay, Billy. Let's get outta here before the fighting catches up with us."

Billy jumped up, wiped the worst of the chicken blood off his face, and pushed through the door. Jaime followed him out into the sunlight.

"Wait!" Billy shouted before ducking back into the chicken coop. He reappeared holding the rooster by its feet. He had to cock his arm to keep the bird from dragging on the ground. He crowed, "Thank You, Jesus, fer savin' my life. And thank You, Jesus, fer givin' us somethin' other than hard tack to eat tonight!"

Someone must have seen or heard them from down the hill because the whiz of minié balls around them returned with a vengeance. There was no halting to reload and return fire this time. The two boys didn't stop running until they had crossed through the newly reformed gray lines on the far side of the hill where their camp lay undisturbed.

That night around the campfires, word went around that Commanding General Johnston had been seriously wounded. A new leader had taken command of the Army of Northern Virginia, a General Robert E. Lee.

Another day's fighting brought an inconclusive end to the battle with both sides claiming victory and roughly an equal number of casualties. Lee set his army to throwing up earthworks to protect nearby Richmond from further attack.

Union General McClellan was shaken and discomfited over the failure of what he had hoped would be the fall of Richmond and a quick end to the war.

Chapter 7

Fire and Ice

Thursday, March 12, 1863

"You look nice, Lizzie." Jaime voiced the first thought that came to mind. It was the first time in months he had seen her other than in the warm memories he always carried with him. Lizzie looked down at her simple blue calico dress, more appropriate for working in the barn than for receiving guests. She responded simply, "Thank you, Jaime."

They were seated once again on the steps of her home, Lizzie one step above Jaime to make up for their difference in height. The silence that hung over them was at once awkward, but comfortable. The comfort came from being near each other again, the awkwardness from not sharing what they were feeling.

"You've lost some weight," Lizzie ventured, not sure how much to ask about his activities.

"Yeah, they don't feed us very well." Jaime shrugged as one who had accepted life as it was. "Mostly, we have to forage for anything we eat. Sometimes, we eat pretty good, but for the most part there's not so much."

Lizzie jumped up, ran inside, but quickly bounced back out the door with half a loaf of rye bread. "I made this yesterday. Still pretty fresh," she commented before tossing the bread to the surprised young man who grabbed it as though it was gold. He tore off a chunk and bit into it with delight in his eyes.

"Mmmm... Ya know Mother fixed me a big supper when I got home last night, but I declare I could eat the whole day long and not get full." Jaime offered the torn loaf back to Lizzie. A forgotten warmth returned to his voice. "So sorry to hear about your mother."

Lizzie nodded, dropping her eyes to her lap as she tore off a tiny piece of bread and nibbled at it. "Thank you... She went much quicker than Doctor Caldwell had thought. He told us later that consumption is worse if the person has a weak heart."

Jaime looked up at her. "I didn't know she had any problems with her heart."

"We didn't either." Lizzie's lower lip started to quiver. Tears filled the corners of her eyes and spilled down her cheeks. Jaime hopped up a step, unsure if he should put his arm around the young woman he cared so much for. Finally, he gently placed his rough hand over hers, saying nothing. Any awkwardness between them washed away like the summer rain falling on the eaves of a well-built house.

Lizzie's words broke the long quiet moment. "Everything keeps changing so much. We never know who is in charge. One day, the Yankees occupy the valleys. The next we watch General Lee's army marching through. There is no real law. We are left to defend ourselves. Nothing is safe. We have hidden our stores of foodstuffs. They aren't safe from either side."

Lizzie continued, "You remember our brown Jersey, Roberta?" Jaime nodded, recalling the early mornings when he rushed through his own chores to help Lizzie with mucking the barn stalls and milking Roberta. "She disappeared a month ago. Papa found what was left of her at the edge of the west field. Whoever stole her only took about half of her and left the rest to rot!" Angry fire smoldered in the young woman's eyes. She pulled her hand back from under his, unconsciously clenching her hands into fists. "Jaime, how much longer will this go on? Both sides claim God is on their side. Someone has got to be wrong!"

Jaime nodded, afraid to give voice to the nagging doubt growing in own his heart.

"You're going back to your regiment soon, aren't you?" Lizzie's words were more of an accusation than a question. Jaime looked at her, fire catching in his own eyes. "You know I have to. I am no deserter, regardless of how I might feel."

The warm rain of caring between them quickly turned into a hailstorm with both Jaime and Lizzie contributing to the supply of ice.

Fifteen minutes later, Jaime stormed down the path to his home. He found his father seated at the sharpening wheel, pedaling left, right, left, right to keep the large stone spinning sufficiently to put a new edge on the old axe. He kept the wheel under the shadow of a live oak, out of the sun. Bright sparks flew from the contact of rock and steel. Jaime stood silently watching his father lean into his work. Finally, his father stopped pedaling and let the wheel spin to a stop.

"Come here, Son. I have something for you." John Winberry stood and led his boy into the harness shed. Jaime had spent a good part of his youth doing chores in the shed. The smells and shadows were familiar friends. He quickly noticed the small, round object hanging on by a nail on a barn post. As his father took it down and handed to him, Jaime realized it was a wooden drum canteen about eight by three inches. The canteen was held together by two iron hoops that bound small slats to the slightly domed sides. Tiny tin guides secured a canvas sling in place. It was topped off by a carved wooden stopper with a leather strap that kept it connected to the canteen. It was the work of a skilled cooper, a barrel maker.

Carved into one side was a large *W* with a smaller *J* and an *A* on either side of that. On the other side, near the bottom, was more carving: *John 4:10*. Jaime thought for a moment before asking, "Living water?"

His father smiled, "Living water, Son."

Later that night, Jaime told his friend seated across the table about the canteen. "I don't know of anything my father has done for me that has meant more. Ya know, when you layin' out in da sun waiting fer da fightin' ta start, a body gets mighty tirsty." Jaime stopped himself with a smile, realizing he was talking like Billy Ott.

Henry said nothing as though he knew there was something else on the young soldier's mind.

"Henry, I wish I could explain it to her."

"Explain it to whom?" queried his black friend.

"Lizzie, uh, Elizabeth Anne." Then, as if he were explaining it to her, Jaime continued, "It's like I live in two rooms. Most of the time I live in the front room with everything and everyone I know and love. But when I go into battle I stand up, walk into the other room, and shut the door. In there I do things I would never do in my front room. I fight, shoot, and kill people I know nothing about except that they are trying to do the same thing to me."

"You know, she loves you, Jaime," the old man replied, cutting directly to the heart of Jaime's worries. The two friends talked through the night, but "she loves you" were the only words that stayed with the young soldier when he opened his eyes the next morning.

Chapter 8

Nothing More Important

Friday, May 15, 1863

Jaime held the letter from his mother in the spot of afternoon sun that made its way through a break in the thick foliage of the maple tree that stood over his bedroll. He recognized the flowing script of her handwriting, the way the letters inclined to the right, all at the same angle as if they had been laid out with a straightedge. The *f*'s, *b*'s, and *h*'s began with a subtle lift and flourish that reminded the young man of the Irish lilt of his mother's voice. Mother wrote her firstborn faithfully. Jaime had just received two letters last week, and it surprised him to receive another so soon. The anticipatory smile on his lips quickly disappeared as he read her words.

April 17, Loudoun County, Commonwealth of Virginia

To my Jaime Love,

It breaks my heart to send you word of your father's passing. I, your brother, Jeremiah, and your sister, Mary, are safe and whole. Your father and Elijah Houghton were up by Loudoun Heights to sell a couple of Elijah's hogs Friday of last week when fighting broke out. An artillery shell burst near them. We are not sure which side fired the shot, just that it fell far from the battle lines. Mercifully, it took Elijah immediately, but left John terribly wounded.

(Jaime could feel the anguish in her words. Mother never referred to Father by his proper name before the children.)

Surgeons did what they could for him. Thank God, the wagon and mules were neither harmed by the fighting nor conscripted by General Lee. A Private Pickerel of the Fifth Virginia brought John home in it. The young man told me he had been in many of the same battles as Eighth but had yet to make your acquaintance.

John was unconscious when the wagon arrived. Private Pickerel helped me get him into bed. He revived when I changed his bandages and was able to tell me about Elijah. He then became very animated and called Jeremiah and Mary to his side. He said in a clear voice, "Listen to me, my children, my loves! There's nothing more important! Nothing more important than serving Jesus!" I wish you could have seen the smile on his face as your brother and sister both agreed with him. Your father must have known he had finished his race. He passed during the night.

Lizzie has agreed to stay with us for now. I sent Jeremiah for her as soon as we got your father settled. She was shaken by the news of her papa, but you know she has strong roots. Right away, she began planning what do to with their animals and crops while she is with us. We put her in your bed in the loft. She tried to conceal her grief, but I awoke during the night to the sound of her crying. It was then I discovered that John had gone to be with his Redeemer.

Jaime's tear-blurred eyes could read no further. Deep within the young soldier something broke. It felt as if he had been sitting on the branch of his live oak back home when it gave way, and now he was falling with it. His grief-stricken heart flailed away, looking for something to grab onto. He felt dizzy and hot at the same time. The son of a pastor had often pictured what would happen if he were to die in battle. His father would stand over his grave, reading from the Bible, giving comfort to family and friends, but never this. Never this!

Jaime found himself two campfires down at Sergeant Bybee's tent. It was an open secret that the bottle of hair oil Bybee's mother regularly sent to him contained about two fingers of olive oil on top of almost a quart of whiskey. The grieving man grabbed the bottle from a surprised Sergeant Bybee's hand and took a pull.

The next hours were an unconscious daze until Jaime lifted his head from the table he knew so well. The old brown Bible lay unattended in the middle. Henry's chair was empty. "Henry?" the young man called, looking around for his friend. The dreamer rose from his chair to look behind him and around the room. "Henry!" he called out again, panic lifting the volume of his voice. James Allen Winberry felt an aloneness such as he had never experienced before. He had never realized how dark the room was around him, nor wondered how the table and chairs were illuminated. But what had always felt warm and inviting now seemed strange and isolated.

Jaime sat once again in the faded blue chair. It now felt uncomfortable, as if he were sitting in another man's seat. "Oh, Jesus," he prayed as if for the first time in his life. "Oh, Jesus, I have always relied on my father's faith, on my father's prayers." Jaime paused, considering carefully his next words. "I've got to know that You are with me. I can't ... I can't do this on my own!" His head bowed and rested on his hands on the table which tipped slightly to the left under the weight of his arms.

If one can fall asleep in a dream, the heartbroken soldier rested for what seemed like hours. Yet at some point he became aware of the weight of a hand laid on his shoulder and of a weight that lifted from his heart. He stayed still, not wanting to lose the sense of peace that had enveloped his exhausted and empty heart.

Finally, he looked up and called out one more time, "Henry?"

"Who be Henry?" Billy Ott's voice answered. Jaime opened his eyes to find himself stretched out on his own bed roll. Billy was seated beside him with a worried look on his face.

"How did I get here, Billy?"

"Well, I got ta worryin' 'bout ya. So I wen' lookin' an' 'bout fell over ya by Sr'gent Bybee's fire. I brung ya back over, but ya he'ped me. Ya had to. I culdn't ha done it by myse'f." Billy's face took on a puzzled look. "Now, Jaime, you and I both know that ya don' drink. Wha' ya go doin' tat fer?"

Jaime lay his forearm across his eyes. His head ached, and his mouth felt like it was full of sawdust. "I just learned my father was killed by a stray artillery shell," he slurred.

Billy's blue eyes filled with tears. He sat by his friend for the next several minutes saying nothing. Every so often the boy-soldier tossed another stick or two onto the fire to keep it alive.

Jaime suddenly sat up and, in agitation, began to feel around his bedding and the ground. "Where is it?" he cried.

"Wat'd ya lose?" Billy asked, alarmed.

"My mother's letter!" Jaime got up on his knees to search around the fire ring.

"I got it, Jaime. Ya dropped it next to the fire. Here." Billy held the slightly crumpled paper out to his friend who grabbed it and looked at Billy askance. "Did you read it?!"

Billy dropped his head, "Nah, Jaime, I can' read wort a spit. An' I wuldn't look at sumthin' from yer ma nohow."

"Sorry, Billy," Jaime apologized as he moved back over to his bedding. "You've been a good friend."

Billy yawned, stretched out on his own blankets and replied, "You da onliest friend that I got in this worl'. I'd do 'bout anyting fer ya." Billy yawned again and became still.

Jaime sighed as he closed his eyes, hoping to get some sleep in what was left of the night. "And I would do the same for you. I guess I'm not so alone after all. G'night, Billy."

The only answer he received was a soft snore.

Chapter 9

Gettysburg

Tuesday, June 30, 1863

Jaime looked to his left, not surprised that his shadow, Billy Ott, stood next to him for muster with a smile on his face that could have lit up a cave.

Today was a first in many ways. The Army of Northern Virginia had made its first foray deep into Pennsylvania. The muster roll call was the first in weeks for the Bloody Eighth. That's what the regiment was called now after so many battles: Manassas two times, Ball's Bluff, Seven Pines, Malvern Hill, Ox Hill, Sharpsburg. Jaime shivered at the memory of the place the Yankees called Antietam. Thousands had died, more had been wounded. After the battle, the regiment had camped by a small creek. Jaime, now a veteran combatant, had removed his shirt to bathe in the stream and found that his right arm was battered and bruised from his wrist to his shoulder, so sore he could hardly move it. He had lost count of the number of times he had fired. His gun had become so hot he had been forced to exchange it back and forth for that of a fallen comrade.

Jaime marveled at how few had lined up for roll call, less than 250 of the original 750 volunteers who had formed the Eighth Virginia Infantry three years before. He was one of the few who had not been wounded, yet. Even Billy carried the scar of a saber slash on his left shoulder, a gift from a charging Union calvary officer. Oh, and the remaining half of his left ear gave testimony to how close that officer had come to taking Billy's young life. It made Billy's smile that morning look all the more twisted.

This was the first morning of Billy's new life. The events of the previous day danced through Jaime's mind. After another exhausting march north through Pennsylvania, the Eighth had encamped for the night just outside of Chambersburg.

Billy had asked, "Jaime, culd you give me a drink from yur canteen? My throt is so scratchy, I culd sharpen my knife on it." Jaime had tossed the canteen to the boy who took a long drink and then examined the container. "Deese yur leters? Dis *W* is fer Winberry, right? But wat's dis *J-O-H-N-4-1-0* on de utter side?" Billy asked.

"My Father carved that for me, Billy. That's John 4:10: "If thou knewest the gift of God, and who it is that saith to thee, Give me to drink; thou wouldest have asked of him, and he would have given thee living water." Jaime quoted from memory.

"Wat's dis livin' water?" Billy questioned.

"Well, Jesus was talkin' about himself. If you believe He is God, that He died for your sins, and that He rose from the dead, He will fill you up like it was the best water. You will never get thirsty again, at least not on the inside." Jaime surprised himself with his answer.

"Do you believe, Jaime? Is tat why yu been a-prayin' fer me? I wunt tat water! Wat do I gotta do?" Billy's words spilled out, jumbled together, but his bright blue eyes revealed the intention of his heart.

"Well ..." Jaime was thinking hard about what his father would say. "You gotta believe, and I guess you need to be baptized."

Billy Ott jumped to his feet and grabbed his friend's hand. "C'mon!"

"Where we goin', Billy?" Jaime asked, letting the boy pull him up.

"Down da hill to Conochek, Conocoche ... What's it called?"

"Conococheague Creek," Jaime answered, still not understanding.

"Yeah, tat! C'mon! Yu gonna put me under." Billy still held his friend's hand and stepped out.

Jaime held up and pulled his hand back. "Wait, wait! I can't do that. You need a preacher, one of the chaplains to baptize you."

Billy's hands went to his waist and he looked up at Jaime. "We ain't seen no chaplin or preacher since I don' know when. We gotta do dis now, afore we get back ta fightin'. An' yu been prayin' to Jesus 'bout me anyhow."

Jaime looked at his friend. Billy was right, and something deep within pushed him powerfully to accede to the young soldier's desperate desire.

Billy Ott again grabbed his baptizer's hand and dragged him down the hill and through the brush that bordered Conococheague Creek. Together, they waded out till the water was waist high on Billy. The bottom mud oozed up between their unclad toes and covered their ankles.

"What do we do now?" Billy looked up expectantly into Jaime's face, his own beaming.

Jaime looked around to make sure they were alone, once again thinking hard. His father's words came back to him. "Do you believe that Jesus Christ is the Son of God?" he asked.

Billy nodded furiously.

"Billy, ya got ta say it," Jaime instructed.

"Yes, yes, I believe!"

"Do you believe He died for your sins and rose on the third day?"

"Yes, I do!"

"Then I baptize you in the name of the Father, the Son, and the Holy Ghost… Now, Billy, hold your nose and bend your knees while I put you under." And with that James Allen Winberry had pushed William Baxter Ott by the shoulders almost straight down into the muddy Conococheague. Billy had come out of the water with a silly grin on his face that had still not faded by the next morning.

Four days later Jaime lay prostrate and unconscious in a hospital wagon, one of hundreds of wagons carrying the wounded of the defeated Army of Northern Virginia south. His right leg had been pierced by grapeshot fired from a Union cannon; his head was fevered from the infection that had set into the wound.

The Eighth Virginia had been positioned on the far-right flank of what was supposed to be Pickett's charge and the taking of Cemetery Ridge. In one hour that charge had turned into a slaughter of incredible proportion. Half of General Pickett's division was killed or captured. Jaime was one of the fortunate ones who made it back to Confederate lines. Billy Ott's body rested just in front of the low stone wall called "The Angle" from which Union infantry had repelled the rebel charge.

Jaime blinked back hot tears as Henry sat down across the table.

Henry was silent until the soldier shifted his elbow onto the left corner of the table, bringing it level once again. "How are you doing, Son?" Henry's voice and eyes were full of compassion.

The dreamer's initial reaction was surprise that Henry was acting as if Jaime's last visit to the table alone had never happened. Jaime leaned back in his chair, realizing that once again the three back slats fit his body perfectly. Then the events of the previous days poured through his memory like a river out of its banks in early spring, cold and overwhelming.

"I ... I lost him, Henry."

"Lost who?" asked the old man with the beginnings of a smile on his face.

"Billy Ott, Henry," Jaime replied hopelessly, his chin dropping to his chest. "I lost Billy Ott!"

"Billy Ott? Jaime, look at me!" Henry's command made the young man lift his eyes. "How could you lose someone who isn't lost?" Henry's chuckle grew into laughter that danced around the room and resonated deep within Jaime's heart.

The wounded man's eyes popped open, and a silly grin ran across his face.

Chapter 10

Talking to You

Thursday, January 14, 1864

Jaime stomped the snow off his feet before entering the eight-by ten-foot wooden shanty he shared with three other soldiers. Winter quarters. After Billy's death, he hadn't wanted to get too close to any of his roommates. Harry Sumpter, George Martin, and Jonathan Moore were all good men. Georgie's family lived near Leesburg, but Jaime just couldn't put himself through the pain and emptiness of making, then losing, another close friend.

Not that there was any fighting during the snow and cold of January. Both armies were focused on the unending battle against frostbite, hunger, disease, and boredom. Every morning began with a chorus of coughs that rose from the chests of men and boys lighting campfires with anything combustible they could find.

Jaime considered himself fortunate compared to many of the other enlisted men. Mother had sent him Father's greatcoat, two sets of faded red long johns, and four pair of socks. He shared his socks with Harry, Georgie, and Jonny but wore both pairs of long johns under his pants and shirt.

The soldiers of the Army of Northern Virginia wore a hodgepodge of whatever clothing they could come up with. Many were clothed thanks to the fallen soldiers of the Army of the Potomac. Others wrapped themselves in blankets or anything that would cut the biting cold.

Dysentery, typhoid fever, malaria, pneumonia, and surprisingly, measles took more lives than all the battles combined. Jaime had been laid up three times over the past three years, never really sure why. This winter found him recovered from his Gettysburg wounds and relatively healthy.

The military solution for boredom was to drill. Every morning after muster, squads, then companies would march and turn, practicing for about an hour before moving into regimental levels of drills and parades. Soldiers also rehearsed the procedures in the Manual of Arms. Every foot soldier could recite the steps of loading and priming his rifle in his sleep, and Jaime was convinced that it was either Jonny or Harry who did so nightly.

Many on both sides of the war threw down their arms and deserted. No one had expected the war to go on so long. What was left of the Eighth Virginia had been transferred to the Richmond area for the defense of the capitol. Most deserters didn't have far to go to reach loved ones. The temptation to escape the cold wooden boxes for the warmth of well-built hearths and real food was too much for too many. Sentries walked the perimeters of encampments more to keep soldiers in than to keep out any enemy foolish enough to brave the cold and wet.

"Halt! Give the countersign!" Jaime challenged the hint of movement and rustle in the bushes about five yards to his right. Thick clouds had obscured the moon, leaving the private to walk his late-night post in the woods north of the encampment mostly by memory.

A frightened whisper answered, "Jaime, is that you? Please don' give me away!"

"Harry? Harry what are you doing?" Jaime lowered his voice so the corporal of the guard wouldn't hear.

"Jaime, I jus' can' take it no mo. My family lives in Louisa, not forty miles from here. I'm goin' home."

"You know what they will do if they catch you!"

"That's why I looked for you, Jaime. Give me a break, Jaime, for the love of God!"

Jaime hesitated. Part of him wanted to lay down his own rifle and join Harry. The other part, the wiser part, knew that the chances of Harry making his way past the other sentries, not to mention the other bivouacking regiments were slim. And if caught,

Harry might confess to Jaime's help no matter what he did.

Finally, the young sentry replied, "Okay, Harry. I'm gonna count to five, then I'm gonna shoot and call for the corporal of the guard. No! Don't say nothin'! Just run!"

A rattling in the bushes sounded like Harry had tripped over something getting away, so Jaime waited an extra second before he started counting, each number spoken a little louder than the preceding. "One, two, three, four, FIVE." He took a deep breath before pointing his weapon toward the ground and pulling the trigger. Boom! The blast shattered the still night. "Corporal of the Guard! Corporal of the Guard!"

Twenty-four hours passed before Jaime was able to lay his head down. He was so tired he doubted he would see Henry.

"But that's the thing about dreams, Jaime. The deeper you sleep, the better you dream, and the better you rest. So really, I'm helping you out."

Jaime laughed. "I guess you're right... Do you think Harry made it? Lots of people desert. Not that many who get caught wind up being shot. But a little more than a year ago General Jackson shot three deserters right in front of their open graves, and they fell right in. I didn't see it, but I talked to someone from that regiment who did. You think he made it?"

"I couldn't say, Jaime. I hope he did. It would be a terrible thing if he got caught. I suspect it's gonna be a terrible thing these next days and weeks, hiding out, making his family carry the load for keeping him safe."

Jaime nodded. "I'm glad I didn't go with him. The thought sure crossed my mind though."

"I reckon it did, Son. But you didn't take off, and I am glad for that too."

Jaime looked intently into the eyes of the man who in some strange way had become a friend and mentor. "But, Henry, I fight for the Confederacy. That means ..."

"Son, over the years people have fought wars, battles, and struggles that in the end they wished they had never gotten involved with."

Jaime focused his attention for the first time on his apparel. The dreamer had never noticed before that he was dressed in the same tan canvas trousers he had put on every day when he was a youth. Buttons, front and back, anchored suspenders that stretched over the simple brown cotton shirt that he had left hanging on the wooden peg beside his bed the day he signed up with the Eighth Virginia. Jaime wore neither hat nor shoes. He bore no visible evidence of being a soldier.

"Henry, how do you see me? Am I your enemy? Am I God's enemy?"

"I consider you to be my friend, James Allen Winberry. Who you are to God is between you and Him, I guess."

Jaime broached the question that had haunted him for so long, "You know, I keep waiting for God to talk to me like He talked to Great-Grandpa Hezekiah. I pray every morning before gettin' outta my sack. And I pray, oh how I call on His name every time I come under fire."

Henry's fingers drummed on the brown Bible under his hand. "Are you sure He isn't talking to you?" His question hung in the air like a maple leaf, whirling on a gust of wind.

"Well, I just wish ..."

And Jaime opened his eyes to the sound of the drummer beating call to morning muster. His friend Henry's deep voice echoed in his mind: *"Are you* sure *He isn't talking to you?"*

Chapter 11

Two Masters

Sunday, June 12, 1864

"Henry, you never told me about those marks on your wrists." Jaime pointed at the noticeable scar on his friend's right wrist. Henry lifted his arm. The cuff of his rough woven shirt dropped to reveal and highlight the difference between the dark ring around his wrist and the skin above and below it.

"Why do you ask, Son?" Henry's voice betrayed no apprehension or threat.

"Well, you know I just came off six days on the line. I heard Sergeant Bybee saying that the Battle of Cold Harbor will be remembered as Grant's

greatest defeat." Jaime paused to run his fingers through his hair as he collected his thoughts. Cold Harbor was for the Yankees what Gettysburg had been for General Lee's army. Thousands of blue-uniformed soldiers had been cut down as they tried to advance against the dug-in gray lines. Though outnumbered two to one, the Confederate army had turned back the massive Union assault. It would have felt like the heady victories of the early days of the war but for the continuing and irreplaceable loss of Confederate officers and soldiers.

Mixed feelings stirred in the heart of the young soldier. The war had been lost at Gettysburg in Jaime's mind. His heart was no longer in it. His feelings against slavery were solidifying with every battle and with every conversation with Henry. But now if the South were to win by some miracle ... The thought hung in his mind like a hornet's nest high in a tree.

"But you are a slave, aren't you?" It was the first time Jaime had directly asked his friend.

Henry dropped his arm and folded his hands together on top of the old Bible. "Jaime, everyone has a master."

The young man forced his open jaw to close. "I … I don't understand."

"You ever remember hearing your father preach on that passage in the Bible, 'No man can serve two masters'?"

"'He will hate the one and love the other,'" Jaime finished the verse. "That's from somewhere in Matthew."

"Well, look at it this way, Son. Jesus taught about two masters. He didn't talk about no master, did He?"

Jaime thought for a moment, then slowly nodded.

Henry looked intently at his friend with penetrating eyes. "Everyone has a master. We all serve someone or something. Have you ever watched Sergeant Bybee when he runs out of his mother's hair oil, how his hands shake, how he gets out of sorts? That whiskey is his master." *Jaime thought of the nights he had seen the sergeant passed out on the ground. He also remembered only too well his own visit to Bybee's fire after learning of his father's death.*

"How about General Lee? Do you think he's truly free? Or is he a slave to this war, answering its every call?" Henry paused to allow his words to sink in before continuing, "There are slaves who are born into bondage. That's a terrible, terrible thing. But so many others put their necks into a yoke of slavery, some knowingly, and others with no idea of what they are doing until it's too late."

Jaime opened his eyes to the call to morning muster. As he stood in the ever-shrinking line of soldiers that made up the Eighth Virginia, he realized that much of his conversation with Henry had stayed with him. All through the day, as companies and regiments moved south to maintain their guard between the Union forces and Richmond, Henry's words played through his mind: "Everyone has a master."

That night saw the gray-clad soldier back on guard duty, this time to the west of the rapidly pitched encampment. Word was that the regiment would cross the James River and continue south to Petersburg in the morning.

Late in the night as the moon was setting and he was about to trudge back up the hill from the river, Jaime heard a low sound, almost a moan. He unslung his rifle and turned toward the disturbance. Silently he approached the source of the sound along the river, ready to call out. As he drew nearer, he began to make out the words of low singing. Peeking from behind a large cottonwood tree, Jaime could see what looked to be nine or ten figures gathered on a gravel bar that paralleled the James River. One sheltered the stub of a candle in her hand. It illuminated the shoulders and neck of an elderly woman, a slave. Her face and those of her companions remained hidden in the shadows, but it was the singing of a single voice that captivated him.

> As I went down in the river to pray,
> Studying about dat good old way,

> When you shall wear de starry crown,
> Good Lord, show me de way.

Then other voices joined the first in almost a chant,

> O mourner, let's go down,
> Let's go down, let's go down,
> O mourner, let's go down,
> Down in the river to pray.

Jaime had to restrain himself from singing with the group when they came to the chorus again, changing the word *mourner* to *brother*. Then he heard a yell from the top of the hill. "Sentinel Guard, Sentinel Guard!" The singing broke off and the candle was snuffed out, plunging the group into total darkness. Jaime could hear feet running across the gravel. He waited to respond until he made his way back up the hill.

The corporal of the guard met him with a lantern in his hand. "Winberry, where were you?!"

Jaime thought furiously. How could he answer truthfully without giving away the group of worshippers? "Corporal, I thought I heard something by the river, so I went down to investigate. Then I heard your call."

"Why didn't you answer me then?"

They were interrupted by another shout, this one closer to the camp. "Corporal of the Guard!"

"Winberry, you stay at your post, and sing out if you see or hear anything. Ya hear me?" Then without waiting for a response, the corporal turned and ran back toward the camp, away from the river.

Jaime let out a relieved sigh and continued his rounds until ordered to return to the camp. Each step he took was in time to the haunting melody that played in his mind: "Let's go down …"

Chapter 12

Five Forks

Saturday, April 1, 1865

The spring rain blurred the vision of marksmen on both sides of the shooting. Jaime could make out movement across the artillery-scarred field that separated the thin line of Confederate defenders from their Union attackers. The blue uniform of the man in his sights would have been almost invisible in the shadows of the trees but for the yellow sergeant's chevron that marked the location just inches to the right of the soldier's heart. Jaime focused his stare on the sergeant as the man stepped out from under the trees and into clearer relief. As another, then another blue-clad fighter stepped out of the trees, Jaime realized two things. Another attack on his position was beginning, and the advancing soldiers were black.

There was a general hatred by Confederate soldiers toward the mostly former slaves who swelled the ranks of Lincoln's armies. They were not treated as enemy combatants, but as stolen property. Policy was to return captives to slavery, but many never survived capture. Jaime flipped from his prone position onto his back, the butt of his rifle resting on the ground, muzzle now pointed to the sky. The sound of gunfire up and down the line increased then diminished as this latest attack was repelled.

"Hold Five Forks at all hazards!" General Robert E. Lee's instructions to General Pickett had filtered down through the ranks. After Gettysburg, hope for the Confederacy had dissipated like smoke from a dying campfire. The Eighth Virginia had lost most of its officers and half its soldiers at Cemetery Ridge. Surviving his own serious wounds, the Eighth's leader, Eppa Hunton, had been promoted to Brigadier General and placed over the remnants of the Eighth,

Eighteen, Nineteenth, Twenty-Eighth, and Fifty-Sixth Virginia Infantry Regiments.

Five Forks protected the last railway and lifeline into Petersburg and Richmond, now under Union siege for nine months. Hunger was rampant. Most people subsisted on cornbread soaked in bacon drippings, dried beans, and hot water with salt or brown sugar sprinkled on it, when it was available. Everyone lived on denial, hope for a miracle victory, reinforcements, anything to grasp on to as the brutal reality of the siege continued its unending crush.

Jaime lay behind the earthworks that he and the ten thousand desperate Confederates under Pickett had thrown up around the Five Forks crossroads to hold back the onslaught of Union attackers. Constant fighting, marching, and digging left him in a state somewhere between asleep and awake, often unable to tell the difference between the two. One moment the weary soldier was talking to Henry, the next he was firing his weapon downfield. When he was awake, opposing thoughts battled for control of his mind.

James Allen Winberry didn't hate these slaves now turned invaders. There was no reservoir of enmity against any of the Union soldiers. At this point he was just trying to survive. The young fighter didn't support slavery although it was obvious he was fighting for it. This war was supposed to be about protecting home and family. Yet thinking back over the past four years was like walking barefoot over freshly broken stone, every edge sharp. Bloody footprints marked the path he had taken. Now he often closed his eyes when he fired his weapon. When he did look, he lifted his aim.

Somewhere deep within him, Jaime had concluded that he and Lizzie would raise their children to treat everyone, regardless of color, with love and respect. If she would have him. Images of Lizzie often popped into his mind, right along with those of his family and of Henry. No, Jesus came to his mind more than anyone nowadays. Baptizing Billy Ott had also buried any doubts about his own faith. It seemed his walk with the Lord now occupied most of Jaime's conversations with Henry ... from what he could remember.

Jaime asked himself, "Why don't you just surrender to the Union?" There was no satisfactory answer. First, he would have to stay alive long enough to get captured. Then, stories of how prisoners of war on both sides were treated were frightening. Maybe it was more his own stubborn pride at having survived battles and evaded capture so far. The end of all of this had to be near. Then what? He would probably wind up in the camps anyway. Jaime sighed and lay his rifle across his lap.

On the other hand, all he had to do was to raise his head high enough above the rim of the muddy trenches, and it could all be over. A Union minié ball would take his life, and he could join Billy. Well, maybe not if he was trying to kill himself. And what about Lizzie and Mother? What would Henry say? Grim determination surged and screwed down the lid on that dark line of thinking. "God, I don't know what to do. I guess just stay alive until You choose to take me!"

As if in response to his prayer, word raced up and down the line. "Sheridan is behind us!" Major General

Phil Sheridan had recently returned with his troops from his punishing drive through the Shenandoah Valley, and now was leading the attack to seal off Richmond. His soldiers had advanced, accidentally bypassing Confederate lines to discover they were in control of north and southbound Ford's Road, effectively cutting off access to Petersburg and Richmond. Pickett's soldiers found themselves in a quickly collapsing bag of Union forces with the only escape being to the northwest. A third of them would be killed or captured.

Jaime dropped everything except his rifle. As he ran, bullets from behind him were replaced by bullets being fired from his left. He stopped to help a fallen comrade, but the man was already dead. The soldier's still warm blood covered Jaime's hands. The next minutes were run, duck or fall, get up and run again. Gradually, the buzz and whiz of minié balls fell off and the defeated soldier slowed to a walk. The pain in his calves and thighs, and the stitch in his side began to subside. Out of habit and drill, the retreating mob around him began to organize itself into marching squads as officers made themselves known.

Pickett's division joined General Johnson's division of North Carolinians who shared the news of the fall of Petersburg. Richmond could not hold out much longer. Officers spoke of meeting with General Lee at Amelia Courthouse.

The next days were full of skirmishes, battles, and bitter disappointments. Hopes for finding rations at Amelia Courthouse were dashed by the empty wagons and railcars that met them. General Sheridan's division paralleled Lee's ragtag regiments as they streamed westward along the Appomattox River.

Every encounter bled the Confederate army of hundreds more, either killed, wounded, or taken prisoner. General Hunton, who had led the Eighth from the beginning, was captured at Sayler's Creek. A last desperate hope for food and supplies now lay at Appomattox Courthouse, a two- or three-day's march beyond them. Jaime's only sustaining hope was his faith in Jesus and his visits with Henry every time he closed his eyes.

Chapter 13

Surrender

Wednesday, April 12, 1865

Sergeant Major William T. McGinnis walked slowly behind the line of small desks facing the mass of bedraggled and defeated men dressed in gray rags. Many were shoeless and all shivered in the early morning mists. He recognized, then ignored, the smell of unwashed bodies, untreated wounds, and death that hung in the air. Sergeant Major McGinnis had seen it all during his nineteen years of service that stretched from the battle of Monterrey in the Mexican-American War through the battles, defeats, and victories of the Army of the Potomac and now here at the last gasp of the Lee's Army of Northern Virginia at Appomattox Courthouse.

It had been three days since General Lee had surrendered his beloved Army of Northern Virginia. The provisions of the surrender were generous. Officers had been allowed to keep their small arms, personal belongings, and mounts. Surrendering soldiers would not be held as prisoners of war, but rather allowed to return to their homes and loved ones.

To McGinnis' left and a step behind strode First Lieutenant Chadwick O. Gilligan. McGinnis looked over his shoulder and sighed. He was grateful that this war was ending, unsure that he had it in him to break in another young officer. They had come and gone so quickly. Several had died foolishly, exposing themselves to Confederate fire in the false assumption that leadership was all about flag and sword waving. Others had been removed for corruption or cowardice. The Sergeant Major had survived by keeping his head down and doing his duty, rising steadily through the ranks. He had twice turned down his own commission, but that was another story.

He glanced anew at Lieutenant Gilligan. The young man showed promise, stepping confidently through the muddy field, silently taking in the transformation of enemy soldiers into farmers and clerks. "Questions, Sir?" McGinnis had to speak over the sound of axes turning a nearby tree into small souvenirs of the rumor that Generals Grant and Lee had paused under its shade to shake hands.

"No, thank you, Sergeant Major." A short pause followed by, "Well, could we speak to a few of the Confederates?"

McGinnis nodded and the two stepped over to the nearest table. Corporal Hiess had just pulled out another freshly-printed parole form, dipped his quill into the slowly-drying inkwell, and waved over another defeated soldier.

"Name and regiment. Last name first, then first name." Hiess' voice had worn to a soft monotone through innumerable repetitions.

The reply came softer still but with a distinct edge of relief. "Winberry, James Allen, Sir. Virginia Eighth Infantry, Sir." Jaime's skin was stretched tight over his tall frame, his cheeks and eyes were sunken after weeks of battle, fighting retreats, and never enough to eat. No one would have guessed that he had yet to celebrate his twenty-third birthday. War had taken its toll on his bruised and unwashed body.

McGinnis looked up at the boy and asked, "The Bloody Eighth? Were you at Bull Run?"

"The first battle of Manassas, you mean, Sir? I was at most all the battles." Jaime's voice hardened at the memory of Billy Ott and so many others now lying quietly in scattered and forgotten graves.

"Don't fret, Son," the Sergeant Major continued, lost for a quick moment in his own memories. "I was wounded and almost captured at Manassas."

Lieutenant Gilligan laid his hand on Corporal Hiess' shoulder and looked at the name being entered on the parole that would guarantee Jaime's passage through Union lines and back home.

"James Allen Winberry." Gilligan focused on the hunched-over young soldier. "Where are you from?" Their eyes met and fixed on each other. Jaime was too exhausted to recognize the compassion in Gilligan's gaze.

"Loudoun County, Sir. Just outside of Leesburg, Sir."

The young lieutenant looked at Jaime with growing interest. "Loudoun County… You ever attend a church there? Ketoctin Baptist Church, I believe it was. The pastor was … was …"

"My father, John Winberry." Jaime's head dropped slightly. "He's gone now."

"I am so sorry to hear that, James," Lieutenant Gilligan replied. "I had wanted to meet him. You may not believe this, but we are family. Did you ever hear of Pastor Hezekiah Smith? He would have been your great-grandfather. He was mine too. My mother was a Smith. I had heard of the Winberry side of the family, but never dreamed I would meet— Is ... is there anything that you need?"

Sergeant Major McGinnis snorted at Lieutenant Gilligan as if the young officer had lost his mind. "Sir, this man has just surrendered. He has nothing!"

"You're absolutely right, Sergeant Major, absolutely right. What can we do?"

Sergeant Major McGinnis stared for a moment at Lieutenant Gilligan. His mind raced back through his years of experience, looking for a reference point he could tie on to. Past prisoners of war, wounded enemies, officers who had circumvented military regulations. Nothing fit finding a lost cousin among enemy combatants. This was a story to be shared at Sergeants' Mess. "Well, Sir. From the looks of him, he could probably use a good meal to start with."

Open mouthed, Jaime looked back and forth between the two strangers who had taken a sudden interest in his welfare. He couldn't grasp the miracle of encountering a cousin who had "randomly" picked him out of the crowd of soldiers. Somewhere in the back of his mind, Henry's words from some night before flashed into his consciousness. "Jaime, it's going to get worse for a bit. Then it's going to get a lot better."

Two days later saw Jaime, cleaned up and with a full stomach, walking toward Appomattox Station. A bittersweet scene greeted him. The supply trains that had awaited Lee's troops had been captured by cavalry under Brigadier General George Custer's command. The loss of armaments, rations, and supplies had been the straw that broke the back of Lee's army. These same trains were now loading Confederate parolees headed east and north.

As he neared the train station the young man marveled at night to day changes in his life. James Allen Winberry's war had finally ended.

"Thank You, Jesus! Thank You, Jesus! Thank You!" Over and over the words poured out under his breath as Jaime looked again and again at the narrow slip of white paper in his hand.

Appomattox Court House, VA.

THE BEARER,

James A. Winberry, Pvt. of Regt of 8th Virginia Infantry,

A Paroled Prisoner of the Army of Northern Virginia has permission to go to his house, and there remain undisturbed.

Signed: Edward A. Flint, Capt. Provost Guard

It was his ticket home. With it, Jaime could obtain rations at Union supply depots. And, importantly, he could use the railroads, now under Union control, for the two-hundred-mile trip back to Loudoun County— back home, back to Mother, back to Lizzie.

Chapter 14

Home Again

Monday, April 17, 1865

Paroled Private James Allen Winberry stepped onto the Harpers Ferry Station platform near the end of his third day of riding Union trains. He looked at the setting sun, deciding to wait till the next day to walk the last fifteen miles home. He had spent the previous two nights stretched out on train platforms under the blanket that newly-discovered Cousin Chadwick had provided for him before they parted ways at Appomattox. Henry had visited the night before while he slept at Richmond station, but as usual, Jaime remembered little more than Henry's deep chuckle and warm eyes.

There were no passenger trains. A few lucky riders had piled into empty freight cars, but most, like Jaime, had ridden on top of the carriages in the wind, the rain, and the near-constant pelting of hot cinders that flew from the smokestacks of the woodburning locomotives. One cinder caught in fellow parolee Jolly Adams' long beard and burned a good-sized hole before someone noticed his beard smoking. Everyone laughed at Jolly's lop-sided face after that. No one had a razor or knife sharp enough to trim it back.

Jaime and his compatriots ate when and where they could. There was usually a supply depot with hard tack and salt pork available near the stations where the riders changed trains. They had been heartened when their train had stopped near a newly-planted sweet potato field. A local farmer's wife had brought them some vegetables to share.

Jaime looked down at the cracked and muddy Brogans on his feet. The heel of his right shoe was gone, and he could stick his big toe through the broken stitching of the sole of his left. They had been in better shape when, after the Battle of Cold Harbor, he took them from the feet of a dead Confederate soldier who had probably lifted them from a Union soldier. He hadn't worn stockings since ... well, he couldn't remember when.

After begging ferry passage across the Shenandoah River the next morning, Jaime walked into Loudoun Heights. The small village was the northern gateway into the rich Shenandoah valley. Loudoun Heights had yet to recover from the ravages of the multiple battles that had waged as each side fought for control of nearby Harper's Ferry and the confluence of the Shenandoah and Potomac Rivers. Jaime pushed thoughts of his father's death here out of his mind.

The silver and sugar maples were already in leaf despite having been scarred, some horribly, by artillery and small-arms fire. Further up the Blue Ridge Mountains on his right and Short Hill Mountain on his left the oaks, hickories, and yellow birch looked as he remembered them. Songbirds filled the air with a mix of trills, warbles, and calls. Jaime stepped out southbound onto Harper's Ferry Road and smiled to himself. Not far now.

Noon brought the young man to Mechanicsville. From there he walked through the fields. He was surprised to find that over half had been plowed and planted. And he was amazed to see black people working in the fields. They were now free, but many had nowhere to go. Yet it seemed to Jaime that there was something different about the way they carried themselves.

"How ironic," the former soldier thought, smiling to himself. "I am rejoicing to see what I spent four years fighting against." He waved at a young black man, probably not much older than himself, passing by on a horse. The man stared back, solemn faced. "It must be my uniform," Jaime mused to himself. "I guess I can't really blame him."

On the other side of an L-shaped field that butted up against the foot of Short Hill Mountain, Jaime could see the roof of Ketoctin Church and maybe, he squinted hard, the roof of his home! He tried to run but the freshly-plowed ground grabbed on to his feet as if it were trying to hold him back. Heart in his mouth, Jaime plodded on until he reached the churchyard.

He could now see the old stand of hickory and live oaks at the side of the cabin. On the other side were two women hanging out laundry. One looked up, screamed, and fell to her knees. The other, shorter, with long brown hair plaited into a braid, turned toward him, leaned slightly to her left, and wrapped her arms around herself.

Martha Taylor Winberry picked herself off the ground and ran to her son. The mother's thin, hard-lined face sparkled with joy. Jaime caught her in his arms, lifted, and spun her around.

"Oh Jaime Love, put your poor mother down and let me look at your face. I've prayed every day for this moment. Are ya home for good?"

Jaime nodded, smiling at her through his tears. "I've been paroled, Mother. For me, the war is over, and I think soon it will be over for everyone."

Martha cupped her hands around her son's face and looked into his eyes, then began sobbing. "I wish your father were here to see this day. He loved you so much, James Allen."

Once again Jaime folded his mother in his arms. He nodded. "I miss him too." They stood for a long quiet moment before she pulled back and exclaimed, "Your brother is working in the garden. We put out a big one this year. Little Mary isn't so little anymore. I think she's in the house if not in the back shed with her kittens." Then Martha stopped herself and looked over her shoulder. "And I expect you'll be wanting to say something to Lizzie. She's been such a help around here."

Jaime released his mother and stepped over to the laundry line where Lizzie stood unmoving, her arms now at her sides. Jaime reached down and brushed aside a brown strand that had escaped the rest of her hair. Lizzie started to say something when her young man wrapped his arms around her and kissed her deeply. Slowly Lizzie's arms came up and rested lightly on his back.

That night Jaime sat in the faded, blue three-slat chair with the woven cane bottom. Across the table was a smiling Henry. "Jaime, I declare your smile is even bigger than mine."

"I suspect you're right, Henry. Well, we made it, didn't we?" Henry nodded in agreement. They sat comfortably for a long moment before Jaime continued. "You know what sticks in my mind more than anything right now? I can still hear Billy Ott when he realized he wasn't shot at Seven Pines, sayin' over and over again, 'Thank You, Jesus! Thank You, Jesus!' That's how I feel. Thank You, Jesus!"

"I'm so glad to hear you say that, Son. You know there's nothing more important than serving the Lord," Henry replied.

Jaime looked thoughtfully at his friend. "That's what my father always said, but you know that don't you?"

"I sure do, I surely do... Jaime, I won't be visiting as often anymore. Now, don't look at me like that. I'll be back from time to time. Sometimes you'll remember, and other times you won't. But it's time for you to get on with your new life, marry that Lizzie, start your own family." Henry's deep chuckle bounced around the room once again.

And with that, Jaime stretched out fully on his bed, opened his eyes, and exclaimed, "Thank You, Jesus!"

Chapter 15

Namesake

June 29, 1913

James Allen Winberry glanced at his pocket watch for the fifth time in as many minutes. He walked back to the front window and looked out at the street again.

A short white-haired woman watched from the kitchen doorway, her arms folded and a half smile on her lips. "Jaime, looking at your watch won't get him here any sooner. You asked Henry to be here at 7:00 this morning. It's only 6:45, and for the life of me, I don't know why you're going to the train station so early!" His wife's chastisement was interrupted by the sound of hoofbeats echoing up the empty brick-paved street.

A buggy stopped in front of the house, and Lizzie Winberry's husband reached for his bag and cane. Lizzie reached for her husband's hat only to watch it being swept away and dropped on her husband's head. "I wish you wouldn't wear that thing, Darlin'. It's falling to pieces. You know, lots of veterans have replaced their old hats and uniforms."

Jaime was already wearing his old battle jacket. It looked like it was one good washing away from completely disintegrating, but the old man wore it with pride. "It was good enough for the war; it'll be good enough for the reunion!"

The man waiting at the door had his father's height and manner, but his mother's face and heart. He hugged his mom, whispering something in her ear before grabbing the small travel bag out of his dad's hand and starting back down the porch steps.

The old man stepped through the door, then hesitated. Lizzie quickly joined him, wrapping her arm around the man with whom she had spent a lifetime. His arm went around her in automatic response, giving her a light squeeze. Jaime started down the steps, but Lizzie held on, unwilling to release her grasp on him. Her husband turned toward the love of his life and pulled her into a full embrace.

They held each other for an eternity of seconds before loosening their mutual hug. Jaime reached down once again to brush back the now gray strand of still recalcitrant hair from Lizzie's face. And once again, unspoken feelings raced back and forth between them.

"Woman, don't you just stand there until that ankle acts up on you again. I'll be fine."

"Old man, I'll stand here as long as I please. Don't you think that you can just lord—" Her words were cut off by an unexpected kiss.

Jaime then turned and slowly walked to the buggy. He struggled a little as he stepped up into the four-wheeled chaise. His son grabbed his right forearm, holding it firmly as his elder worked himself into the seat.

"Thank-ee, Pastor Winberry. I wouldn't want to fall before I even got a block away."

Henry chuckled at their oft-repeated inside joke. "Well, to be honest, Brother James, I was more concerned about what my mother might say come Sunday services than anything else."

Jaime looked over his shoulder to catch a last look at a smiling Lizzie, still standing in the door of their home, leaning slightly to the left to keep the weight off her bad ankle. She answered his wave with a raised hand as the buggy pulled around the block.

Both men sat comfortably, each in his own thoughts for several quiet minutes. "How are the children?" Jaime finally asked without taking his eyes off the automobile that turned onto the street about fifty yards ahead of them.

Henry pulled back on old Billy's reins. "He's still not used to them things, so I'll just hold up for a minute. They're all doing fine, Dad. Ramona is still trying to decide what to do now that she has finished high school. Albert is working at the livery this summer, but he wants to learn how to repair those things." The buggy whip pointed in the direction of the disappearing Model T. "And Lil' Jaime is staying up at Nyack College this summer before finishing up next year. He says he's got a good summer job, but it's more likely that he's sweet on that Andrea girl he's been writing us about. You know, her uncle is one of the professors at the school. I think he teaches Old Testament or something like that."

"That boy still talking about following in his father's footsteps?"

"You know, Dad, 'that boy' did a study on Great-Great … I forget how many 'greats' now … Grampa Hezekiah. But Lil' Jaime says that his own call to be a pastor is between him and Jesus. In his last letter he talked about a move of God on campus that was so strong they canceled classes for a week."

Old Jaime smiled but said nothing further till they came in sight of the train station. The Model T they had seen earlier was parked on the far side of the hitching rail. "You think your mother will be okay without me?"

"Well, according to Mom, she mostly takes care of you these days. She told me that she's lookin' forward to getting through the night without you shoutin' out or jerkin' your legs around in bed."

Jaime smiled again and retorted, "According to your mother, she kept me safe all through the war and fit Genr'l Sheridan to a standstill too."

Silence reigned as Billy pulled up to the hitching post and stopped without Henry moving the reins. "Dad, can I ask you something about the war? I know you don't usually talk about it, but there's something I have always wondered."

Jaime pulled out his watch, opening and closing the cover. Two and a half hours to go before the special to Gettysburg was to stop in Leesburg. The train had been laid on to carry the veterans from both sides of the war to the reunion. He sat for a minute staring at the silver case in his hand. "Son, as much as I can, I will just about tell you anything."

"You know, Dad, you and Mom taught us to respect everyone. What was it you used to say? 'We're all God's children, regardless of what we look like on the outside.'" Henry paused as his father nodded. A faraway look crept over the old man's face. "Dad, you have any regrets about fighting for the Confederacy?"

The old veteran opened the silver case on his watch again, his unfocused eyes not really looking at its white porcelain face. "Henry, did I ever tell you about your namesake?"

The middle-aged pastor jerked back in his seat, so much so that Billy snorted and sidestepped, shaking his reins. Henry soothed the horse with a soft voice, "Easy, Billy, I'm sorry." He turned to his father. "I don't remember anyone named Henry on either side of the family."

His father grimaced a little and replied, "No, I don't suppose you do." He paused. "Henry was my best friend when I was young and through the war. But there's a reason you have never heard of him." For the next two and a half hours, then for another hour until the delayed train finally arrived, Jaime told his son about Henry.

Chapter 16

Reunion

Friday, July 4, 1913

Jaime leaned forward, slid his elbow over to the left corner of the table to hold it down and looked across at his friend.

Henry chuckled and with a deep, almost rumbly, voice said, "Some things never change, do they?"

Jaime laughed, "You know I was just going to say the same. All these years and you haven't changed a bit."

"But you surely have, Jaime. You surely have."

For the next timeless hours, the two friends caught up on old memories that were once again sharp in

Jaime's mind. They laughed anew over Billy's chicken. Jaime mimicked Billy's voice, "Ya know, H'nry. It were da bes' chicken I ever et!" He snorted and took a moment to catch his breath before continuing. "Truth to tell, I've made a lot of friends over the years, but none better ... none better. I miss him."

Henry's warm eyes sparkled with understanding. Finally, he broke the comfortable silence. "I guess you and Lizzie have done pretty well."

A different kind of smile broke out on the old man's face, one of contentment mixed with a little pride. "We did at that. She keeps me straight. It was you and Lizzie that got me through the war ... and Jesus more than anyone."

Henry echoed his friend's words, "More than anyone."

Jaime's eyes slowly pulled back from their embrace of Henry's face, down his shoulder, along his arm and hand to the book that lay before him.

Its brown leather cover was very worn and a little torn from heavy use. He could barely make out the faint gold lettering that read Holy Bible.

"May I?" Jaime asked for the first time, and Henry lifted his scarred wrist from the book. The Bible fell open in the old veteran's gnarled hands to the book of Isaiah. There, a passage was marked— chapter fifty-nine, verse twenty-one:

As for me, this is my covenant with them, saith the Lord; My spirit that is upon thee, and my words which I have put in thy mouth, shall not depart out of thy mouth, nor out of the mouth of thy seed, nor out of the mouth of thy seed's seed, saith the Lord, from henceforth and forever.

In the margin, in faded ink, was the date, August 12, 1773, and the initials H. S.

"Great-Grandpa Hezekiah?" Jaime gasped as all the pieces of the mystery fell into sudden sharp focus. "You mean all of this, our visits, everything that happened is because of a promise to him?"

Henry's chuckle blossomed into a full-throated laugh, his smile flashing in the semi-darkness. "Well, truth to tell, he thought it was. But that promise to your family goes back much farther than him."

Jaime sat in stunned silence. He thought about his mother and father, of Billy Ott, and then of his own children and grandchildren and slowly shook his head. All the prayers he had lifted for them rose from the depths of his mind like a great chorus as he imagined them joining those of his folks, their parents, grandparents, and farther back—all growing into a roar of many waters. A small smile lifted the corners of his mouth, and his eyes lightened.

"Are you Jesus?" he asked his friend of so many years.

Another deep chuckle. "No, but I work for Him." Henry slowly stood and turned toward a door Jaime had never noticed before. As he reached for the door handle, he looked back and asked with a laugh in his voice, "I don't suppose you want to come with me, do you?"

"What about Lizzie?" came the response, quick enough to indicate that the thought had already been on Jaime's mind.

Henry smiled and turned back to the door. "Well, she'll be right along before you know it."

Jaime sprang from his chair, knocking the old table to the side, the years falling off him like old discarded wooden shingles. Henry opened the door, revealing a sight far beyond anything human words could describe. Jaime's smile turned into open-mouthed wonder as he heard a voice with a slight Irish lilt call out, "Ah, Jaime Love ..."

July 5, 1913, began brightly. All the speeches and events were over. Most of the veterans had already left, but a few had spent one more night in the tents. Private Hughes of the US Army's Quartermasters Corps moved methodically from tent to tent, folding cots and chairs and placing them outside for removal before the tents were torn down. He was surprised and a little frustrated to find that one of the old men was still stretched out on his cot. His tattered coat hung underneath his old hat on a faded, blue three-slat, cane-bottomed chair.

"Sir ... Sir! You'll have to get up. We have to tear the tents down this morning."

The only response was a hand that slipped out of the sheets to the ground. Its owner had already departed.

Epilogue

Monday, October 16, 1982

Al tentatively pushed open the door of the third-floor prayer chapel and peeked in. Most of the young residents of Welch Hall had already gone to bed or were studying late into the night. Al stepped into the dimness of the empty room and threw himself down on the green and orange shag carpet. The seventeen-year-old glanced around once more before setting his Big Ben windup alarm clock beside him on the carpet. His watch was broken, and he couldn't afford to replace or repair it.

The preceding weeks had painfully crawled by for Albert James Winberry as he struggled to adjust to his new life at Central Bible College. Mom and Dad had dropped him off on a Saturday in August, the first time he had been away from home for more than a week.

Dorm and class registrations had been a whirlwind of confusing choices. Did he have a roommate? No. One was assigned to him, Kit Burganson. They were to share room 110 on 1 West, a first-floor hall full of other freshmen, most of them just as lost as Al and Kit. The rooms were barely big enough for two twin beds on opposite walls, two dressers, two desks with two chairs with space left over to turn around if the inhabitants took turns. A two-inch rod ran the length of the dorm room just below the ceiling. It passed through every room, ending at either end of Welch Hall with twelve-inch square metal plates and large nuts that held the rod and the building in place.

Al had studiously avoided registering for classes taught by professors with demanding reputations. His high school grades reflected his lack of confidence in his ability to learn. Frankly, he was surprised that CBC had approved his application, and he was scared. His greatest fear was that everyone would discover just how unprepared he was for college. Midterms were coming soon. He had read his textbooks, other assigned reading, and had started two short papers but had no real idea what he was doing.

Al had heard of the prayer chapel from some upper classmen were who were discussing, over supper, the amount of time they devoted to prayer. Prayer—that was what Al needed more than anything. He stared up at the dark wood-paneled walls. Centered on the front wall was a picture of Jesus with long brown hair that flowed into his beard. The image was encased in a brass frame with a small light that hung a few inches above and beyond the picture, illuminating Jesus' face. It was beautiful. It was peaceful. It was the exact opposite of the turmoil the freshman was feeling.

"Oh God, what am I doing here?" Al said, more to himself than to the Lord. His mind drifted back to the Sunday morning church service just over a year before when he felt … no, Al *knew* God had called him to be a minister. The raw emotion of that moment still brought tears to the young man's eyes.

He thought about his Great-Uncle Isaac "Ike" Winberry. Al had never known the man but had gazed at his relative's headstone every time his folks took him along on their visits to the rural family cemetery. Brother Ike was a Missionary Baptist pastor who had planted churches throughout the valleys and hills of Southern Virginia. Several of the churches had gotten together and purchased the headstone for him and his wife, Mary. Under the family name was Uncle Ike's oval picture. He was wearing a black fedora, wire rimmed glasses over a hawk-like nose, a small black bow tie on his white shirt, and a grim set to his lips. Deeply carved block letters formed an arch over his picture that called out to any onlooker: R E P E N T. Uncle Ike had been a silent role model for young Al.

Yet the struggles of this strange place with all its requirements and expectations felt overwhelming to the disheartened student. "God, I've got to know … I've got to know You are with me. Please, give me something. I have never asked for a sign or anything like that before, but I've got to have something!"

Al reached for his Bible. The chocolate brown leather cover was inscribed *Holy Bible* in bright gold leaf. It had been a graduation gift just months before, an investment in his future. He thumbed through its pages before opening it near the middle. The young man looked at the top of the left-hand column on the left page. The words on the page began, "out of the mouth of thy seed, nor out of the mouth ..." Al quickly turned back a page to begin the verse:

"My spirit that is upon thee, and my words which I have put in thy mouth, shall not depart out of thy mouth, nor out of the mouth of thy seed ..."

Somewhere in the heavenlies a deep chuckle bloomed into a full-throated laugh of joy and then was joined by another voice and still another, then even more till they became a mighty roar.

Author's Note

A Promise to be Kept is a work of historical fiction. The main characters are fictional. However, many of the characters as well as all the locations and battles were drawn from historical records. Ketoctin Baptist Church is located in Loudoun County, Virginia not far from Leesburg.

The Bloody Eighth Virginia Infantry was commanded by Eppa Hunton until his capture at Sayler's Creek just before Lee's surrender at Appomattox. Hunton's order to charge the Union lines at Manassas in chapter four along with Corporal Donohoe's letter to his mother were taken from the "Regiment History: 8th Virginia Infantry" (https://www.warofrightsforum.com/showthread.php?5755-Regiment-History-8th-Virginia-lnfantry, accessed 21 Feb 2021)

Billy Ott was based on a picture of PVT William Baxter Ott complete with Bowie knife and rifle in hand. The slaves' song in chapter 11 was taken from

Slaves Songs of the United States, complied by William Allen, Charles Ware, and Lucy Garrison, A. Simpson & Company, New York. 1867.

Finally, Brother Ike Winberry mentioned in the Epilogue is really Isaac Pace who lies with his wife, Mary, at Sandridge Cemetery in rural Cedar County, Missouri under the stone put up by the churches he established. The stone holds his picture and arched words that still declare to all who pass by: R E P E N T. He was my great uncle.